Peter Heins

Cinderella

Or, the little glass slipper: and, Jack and the bean-stalk

Peter Heins

Cinderella
Or, the little glass slipper: and, Jack and the bean-stalk

ISBN/EAN: 9783337322229

Printed in Europe, USA, Canada, Australia, Japan

Cover: Foto ©Andreas Hilbeck / pixelio.de

More available books at **www.hansebooks.com**

THE HISTORY OF CINDERELLA
OR THE LITTLE GLASS SLIPPER

LONDON · PVBLISHED BY J·M·DENT AND Cᵒ

AT ALDINE HOVSE IN GREAT EASTERN ST E·C

· MDCCCXCIV

To Hesper.

———⋀⋀⋀———

LONG ago, when our grandmothers were little and lived in lonely country places, and when books and book-shops were not so plentiful as now, children had to wait for their fairy-tales till the pedlars came round. These pedlars journeyed from place to place through the country, their wares strapped to their shoulders, and many were the wonders to be found in their packs. Not least of them all were the children's chap-books, very small, sold for a penny, with the most delightful paper covers, striped with blue and red. And inside, what pictures! It was from one of these very books that our stories of "Jack and the Beanstalk" and "Cinderella and the little Glass Slipper" came. In its pages, one picture, no bigger than a penny, showed the coach and the six footmen looking just like six ninepins. Another showed Cinderella's sisters dressing for the ball, in the queerest petticoats and the most shocking looks. And another showed Jack climbing a beanstalk whose beans were as big as cabbages.

Though Jack is always an English hero, Cinderella's story has been told in many countries. But whether the god-mother is a fairy bird or an old woman, or whether the naughty sisters chop their toes till they fit into the glass slipper, or not, it is always the same Cinderella, best loved of all the maids in fairy-tale who married princes and lived happy ever after. But what, perhaps, you will ask, as you read her story,—what is a pumpion? I think it must be a pumpkin; but of this I am quite sure, that though you might turn a pumpion into a coach by scooping out the inside, a pumpkin you never could.

GRACE RHYS.

Cinderella, or The Little Glass Slipper.

THERE lived once a gentleman who married for his second wife the proudest woman ever seen. She had two daughters of the same spirit, who were indeed like her in all things. On his side, her husband had a young daughter, who was of great goodness and sweetness of temper; in this she was like her mother, who was the best woman in the world.

No sooner was the wedding over than the step-mother began to show her ill-humour; she could not bear her young step-daughter's gentle ways, because they made those of her own daughters appear a thousand times more odious and disagreeable. So she employed her in the meanest work of the house; she it was who must wash the dishes and rub the tables and chairs, and it was her place to clean madam's chamber and that of the misses, her daughters. She herself slept up in a sorry garret, upon a wretched straw bed, while her sisters' rooms had shining floors and curtained beds, and looking-glasses so long and broad that they could see themselves from head to foot in them.

The poor girl bore everything with patience, not daring to complain to her father. When she had finished her work she used to sit down in the chimney corner among the cinders; so that in the house she went by the name of Cinderwench. The youngest of the two sisters, however, being rather more civil than the eldest, called her Cinderella. But Cinderella, ragged as she was, looked a hundred times more charming than her sisters, decked out in all their splendour.

It happened that the king's son gave a ball, to which he invited all the persons of fashion for miles around; our two misses were among the number, for they made a great figure in the country. They were delighted with this invitation, and were wonderfully busy choosing such dresses as might become them. This was a new

trouble for Cinderella, for it was she who
ironed her sisters' linen, and plaited their
ruffles. There was little then talked of
but what dresses should be worn at the
ball. "I," said the eldest, "will wear
my crimson velvet gown." "I," said
the youngest, "will wear a dress all
flowered with gold and a brooch of
diamonds in my hair." Yet they sent
for Cinderella to ask her advice, for she
had excellent taste. She helped them as
much as she could, and even offered to
dress their hair, which was exactly what
they wanted.

While she was busy over this, her sisters said to her, " Cinderella, should not you be glad to go to the ball?" " Ah," said she, " you but mock me; it is not for such as I am to go thither." " You are in the right of it," replied they, " it would make the folk laugh to see a Cinderwench at a ball." Any other than Cinderella would have dressed their hair awry, but she was good and did nothing but her best.

At last the happy moment arrived: they all set off, and Cinderella looked after them till they passed from her sight, when she sat down and began to cry.

Her godmother came in, and seeing her in tears, asked what ailed her. " I want—oh, I want—" sobbed poor Cinderella, without being able to say another word.

Her godmother, who indeed was a fairy, said to her, " You want to go to the ball, isn't it so?" " Oh, yes!" said Cinderella, sighing. " Well then," said her godmother, " be but a good

girl, and I will contrive that you shall
go."

Then taking her kindly by the hand,
she said " Run now into the garden, and
bring me a pumpion." Cinderella flew
at her bidding, and brought back the
finest she could get. Her godmother
scooped out the inside, leaving nothing
but the rind; this done, she struck it with

her wand, and the pumpion was instantly
changed into a fine coach, gilded all over
with gold. She then went to look into
the mouse-trap, where she found six mice,
all alive ; she told Cinderella to raise the
door of the mouse-trap, and as each
mouse came out, at one tap of her wand
they changed into splendid horses ; so
that now Cinderella had a coach and six
horses of a fine dappled mouse-colour.
"Here, my child, are your coach and
horses," said the godmother ; " but what

shall we do for a coachman ? run and see if there be not a rat in the trap;" Cinderella brought the trap, and in it were three huge rats. The fairy made choice of the biggest of the three, and having touched him, he was turned into a fat jolly coachman, who mounted the hammer-cloth in a trice.

She next said to Cinderella—"Go again into the garden, and you will find six lizards behind the watering-pot; bring them hither." She had no sooner done so, than her godmother turned them into smart footmen, who at once skipped up behind the coach.

Then said the fairy, "Now, then, here is something that will take you to the ball ; are you pleased with it ?" "Oh, yes," cried she, "but must I go in these dirty clothes ?"

Her godmother only touched her with her wand, and her clothes were turned into cloth of gold and silver, all beset with jewels. This done, she gave her a pair of glass slippers, the prettiest in the world.

B

Being thus decked out, she got into her coach ; but her godmother bade her, above all things, not to stay past midnight, telling her that if she stayed a single moment longer, all her fine things would return to what they had been before.

She promised her godmother she would not fail to leave the ball before midnight, and then away she drove.

The king's son, being told that a great princess had come, ran out to receive her ; he gave her his hand as she stepped from her coach, and led her among all the company.

Cinderella no sooner appeared than every one was silent ; both the dancing and the music stopped and then all the guests might be heard whispering, " Ah, how handsome she is." All the ladies were busied in gazing at her clothes and head-dress, that they might have some made after the same pattern. The king's son took her to dance with him : she danced so gracefully that they all more and more admired her.

A fine supper was served up, whereof the young prince ate not a morsel, so intently was he busied in gazing on her. She sat down by her sisters, giving them part of the fruit which the prince had presented her with; which very much surprised them. While Cinderella was thus talking with her sisters, she heard the clock strike eleven and three-quarters, whereupon she immediately made a curtsey to the company and then hastened away. Being got home, she thanked her godmother, and said she could not but wish she might go next day to the ball, because the king's son had desired her.

While she was telling her godmother all that had passed, her two sisters knocked at the door, and Cinderella opened. "How long you have stayed!" cried she, pretending to yawn. "If you had been at the ball," said one of them, "let me tell you, sleepiness would not have fallen on you. There came thither the very handsomest princess ever seen with eyes; she shewed us a thousand

kindnesses, and gave us oranges and citrons." Cinderella asked the name of the princess, but they told her they did not know it, and that the king's son was uneasy, and would give all the world to know who she was.

At this, Cinderella, smiling, replied, "She must be very beautiful: could I not see her? Ah! dear Miss Charlotte, do lend me your yellow suit of clothes that you wear every day?"— "Oh, indeed!" cried Miss Charlotte, "lend my clothes to such a dirty Cinderwench as thou art!"

The next day the two sisters went

to the ball and so did Cinderella, dressed still more magnificently than she had been on the first night.

The king's son was always by her, and said the kindest things to her imaginable. She was so far from feeling wearied by this, that she forgot the charge her godmother had given her; so she at last counted the clock striking twelve when she took it to be no more than eleven: she then fled as nimble as a deer. The prince followed, but could not overtake her; she dropped one of her glass slippers, which the prince carefully took up. She got home all out of breath, without coach or footmen, and in her old clothes, having nothing left of all her finery but one of the little slippers. The guards of the gate were asked if they had seen a princess go out, but they said they had seen nobody except a young girl very meanly dressed.

When the two sisters returned, Cinderella asked them if they had been

as much amused as the night before,
and if the beautiful princess had been
there? They told her, yes, but that
she hurried away at twelve o'clock, so
fast that she dropped one of her glass
slippers, which the king's son had taken
up; and that he was surely in love
with the person to whom the slipper
belonged.

What they said was perfectly true,
for the king's son caused it to be
given out that he would marry her
whose foot this slipper would exactly
fit. So they began by trying it on

the princesses, then on the duchesses, and all the court, but in vain; they then brought it to the two sisters, who both tried all they could to force their feet into the slipper, but without success.

Cinderella, who was looking at them all the while, could not help smiling, and said, "Let me see what I can do with the slipper," which made her sisters laugh heartily. "Very likely," said they, "that it will fit your clumsy foot!" The gentleman who was sent to try the slipper saw that she was very handsome, and said he had been ordered to try it on everyone that pleased. Then, putting the slipper to her foot, he found that it went on very easily, and fitted her as though it had been made of wax.

The astonishment of the two sisters was great, but still greater when Cinderella drew out of her pocket the other slipper, and put it on! At that very moment in came her godmother, and with one touch of her wand, made

Cinderella appear more magnificent than ever.

The sisters knew her again at once, and throwing themselves at her feet, begged pardon for the ill-treatment they had made her undergo. Cinderella forgave them with all her heart, and begged they would always love her.

She was then led to the palace where the young prince received her with great joy, and in a few days they were married. Cinderella, who was as good as she was beautiful, took her sisters to live in the palace, and shortly afterwards matched

them to two great lords of the court,
and they all lived happily ever afterwards.

THE HISTORY OF JACK AND THE BEANSTALK.

LONDON · PVBLISHED BY J. M. DENT & Cº

AT ALDINE HOVSE IN GREAT EASTERN ST E C

MDCCCXCIV.

Jack and the Bean-Stalk.

THERE once lived a poor widow, in a cottage which stood in a country village, a long distance from London, for many years.

The widow had only a child named Jack, whom she gratified in everything; the end of her foolish kindness was, that Jack paid little attention to anything she said; and he was heedless and naughty. His follies were not owing to bad nature, but to his mother never having chided him. As she was not rich, and he would not work, she was obliged to support herself and him by selling everything she had. At last nothing remained, only a cow.

The widow, with tears in her eyes, could not help scolding Jack. "Oh!

you wicked boy," said she, "by your naughty course of life you have now brought us both to fall! Heedless, heedless boy! I have not money enough to buy a bit of bread for another day: nothing remains but my poor cow, and that must be sold, or we must starve!"

Jack was in a degree of tenderness for a few minutes, but soon over; and then becoming very hungry for want of food he teased his poor mother to let him sell the cow; which at last she sadly allowed him to do.

As he went on his journey he met a butcher, who asked why he was driving the cow from home? Jack replied he was going to sell it. The butcher had some wonderful beans, of different colours, in his bag, which caught Jack's fancy. This the butcher saw, who, knowing Jack's easy temper, made up his mind to take advantage of it, and offered all the beans for the cow. The foolish boy thought it a great offer. The bargain was momently struck, and the cow exchanged for a few paltry beans. When

Jack hastened home with the beans and told his mother, and showed them to her, she kicked the beans away in a great passion. They flew in all directions, and fell as far as the garden.

Early in the morning Jack arose from his bed, and seeing something strange from the window, he hastened downstairs into the garden, where he soon found that some of the beans had taken root, and sprung up wonderfully: the stalks grew of an immense thickness,

and had so entwined, that they formed a ladder like a chain in view.

Looking upwards, he could not descry the top, it seemed to be lost in the clouds. He tried it, found it firm, and not to be shaken. A new idea immediately struck him : he would climb the bean-stalk, and see whither it would lead. Full of this plan, which made him forget even his hunger, Jack hastened to tell it to his mother.

He at once set out, and after climbing for some hours, reached the top of the bean-stalk, tired and almost exhausted. Looking round, he was surprised to find himself in a strange country ; it seemed to be quite a barren desert ; not a tree, shrub, house, or living creature was to be seen.

Jack sat himself pensively upon a block of stone, and thought of his mother ; his hunger attacked him, and now he felt sorrowful for his disobedience in climbing the bean-stalk against her will ; and made up his mind that he must now die for want of food.

However, he walked on, hoping to
see a house where he might beg something to eat. Suddenly he saw a
beautiful young woman at some distance.
She was dressed in an elegant manner,
and had a small white wand in her

hand, on the top of which was a pea-
cock of pure gold. She came near and
said : "I will tell to you a story your
mother dare not. But before I begin,
I require a solemn promise on your part
to do what I command. I am a fairy,
and unless you perform exactly what I
direct you to do, you will take from me
the power to assist you ; and there is
little doubt but that you will die in the
attempt."   Jack was rather frightened
at this caution, but promised to follow
her directions.

"Your father was a rich man, with
a greatly generous nature. It was
his practice never to refuse help to
the poor people about him ; but, on
the contrary, to seek out the helpless
and distressed. Not many miles from
your father's house lived a huge giant,
who was the dread of the country
around for cruelty and wickedness.
This creature was moreover of a very
envious spirit, and disliked to hear
others talked of for their goodness and
humanity, and he vowed to do him a

mischief, so that he might no longer
hear his good actions made the subject of every one's talk. Your father
was too good a man to fear evil from
others ; so it was not long before
the cruel giant found a chance to
put his wicked threats into practice ;
for hearing that your parents were
about passing a few days with a friend
at some distance from home, he caused
your father to be waylaid and murdered,
and your mother to be seized on their
way homeward.

" At the time this happened, you
were but a few months old. Your
poor mother, almost dead with affright
and horror, was borne away by the
cruel giant's servants, to a dungeon
under his house, in which she and
her poor babe were both long kept
prisoners. Distracted at the absence
of your parents, the servants went in
search of them; but no tidings of
either could be got. Meantime he
caused a will to be found making
over all your father's property to him

as your guardian, and as such he took open possession.

"After your mother had been some months in prison, the giant offered to restore her to liberty, on condition that she would solemnly swear that she would never tell the story of her wrongs to any one. To put it out of her power to do him any harm, should she break her oath, the giant had her put on ship-board, and taken to a distant country; where she was left with no more money for her support than what she got by selling a few jewels she had hidden in her dress.

"I was appointed your father's guardian at his birth; but fairies have laws to which they are subject as well as mortals. A short time before the giant killed your father, I transgressed; my punishment was the loss of my power for a certain time, which, alas, entirely prevented my helping your father, even when I most wished to do so. The day on which you met the butcher, as you went to sell your mother's cow, my power was restored.   It was I who secretly prompted you to take the beans in exchange for the cow.   By my power the bean-stalk grew to so great a height, and formed a ladder.   The giant lives in this country; you are the person who must punish him for all his wickedness.   You will meet with dangers and difficulties, but you must persevere in avenging the death of your father, or you will not prosper in any of your doings.

"As to the giant's goods, every-thing he has is yours, though you are deprived of it; you may take, therefore, what part of it you can.   You must, however, be careful, for such is his love for gold, that the first loss he discovers will make him outrageous and very watchful for the future.   But you must still pursue him; for it is only by cunning that you can ever hope to get the better of him, and become pos-sessed of your rightful property, and the means of justice overtaking him for his barbarous murder. One thing I desire is, do not let your mother know you are aware of your father's history till you see me again.

" Go along the direct road; you will soon see the house where your cruel enemy lives. While you do as I order you, I will protect and guard you; but remember, if you disobey my commands, a dreadful punishment awaits you."

As soon as she had made an end she disappeared, leaving Jack to follow his journey. He walked on till after sunset, when, to his great joy, he espied a large mansion. This pleasant sight revived his drooping spirits; he redoubled his speed, and reached it shortly. A well-looking woman stood at the door: he spoke to her, begging she would give him a morsel of bread and a night's lodging. She expressed the greatest surprise at seeing him; and said it was quite uncommon to see any strange creature near their house, for it was mostly known that her husband was a very cruel and powerful giant, and one

that would eat human flesh, if he could possibly get it.

This account terrified Jack greatly, but still, not forgetting the fairy's protection, he hoped to elude the giant, and therefore he begged the woman to take him in for one night only, and hide him where she thought proper. The good woman at last suffered herself to be persuaded, for she had a kind heart, and at last led him into the house.

First they passed an elegant hall, finely furnished; they then went through several spacious rooms, all in the same style of grandeur, but they seemed to be quite forsaken and desolate. A long gallery came next; it was very dark, just large enough to show that, instead of a wall each side, there was a grating of iron, which parted off a dismal dungeon, from whence issued the groans of several poor victims whom the cruel giant kept shut up in readiness for his very large appetite. Poor Jack was in a dreadful fright at witnessing such a horrible scene, which caused him to fear

that he would never see his mother, but
be captured lastly for the giant's meat;
but still he recollected the fairy, and
a gleam of hope forced *itself into his
heart.

The good woman then took Jack to a
large kitchen, where a great fire was
kept; she bade him sit down, and gave
him plenty to eat and drink. When
he had done his meal and enjoyed
himself, he was disturbed by a hard
knocking at the gate, so loud as to

cause the house to shake.   Jack was
hidden in the oven, and the giant's wife
ran to let in her husband.

Jack heard him accost her in a voice
like thunder, saying : " Wife ! wife ! I
smell fresh meat ! "   " Oh ! my dear,"
replied she, " it is nothing but the people
in the dungeon."   The giant seemed to
believe her, and at last seated himself

by the fireside, whilst the wife prepared
supper.

By degrees Jack managed to look at
the monster through a small crevice.
He was much surprised to see what an
amazing quantity he devoured, and
supposed he would never have done
eating and drinking. After his supper
was ended, a very curious hen was
brought and placed on the table before
him. Jack's curiosity was great to see
what would happen. He saw that it

stood quiet before him, and every time the giant said : " Lay ! " the hen laid

an egg of solid gold. The giant amused himself a long time with his hen ; meanwhile his wife went to bed. At length he fell asleep, and snored like the roaring of a cannon. Jack finding him still asleep at daybreak, crept softly from his hiding - place, seized the hen, and ran off with her as fast as his legs could possibly carry him.

Jack easily found his way to the bean-stalk, and came down better and quicker than he expected. His mother was overjoyed to see him. "Now, mother," said Jack, "I have brought vou home that which will make you rich." The hen laid as many golden eggs as they desired ; they sold them, and soon · had as much riches as they wanted.

For a few months Jack and his mother lived very happy, but he longed to pay the giant another visit. Early one morning he again climbed the bean-stalk, and reached the giant's mansion late in the evening : the woman was at the door as before. Jack told her a pitiful tale, and prayed for a night's shelter. She told him that she had admitted a poor hungry boy once before, and the little ingrate had stolen one of the giant's treasures, and ever since that she had been cruelly used. She however led him to the kitchen, gave him a supper, and put him in a lumber closet. Soon after the giant came in, took his supper, and ordered his wife to bring down his bags of gold and silver. Jack peeped out of his hiding-place, and observed the giant counting over his treasures, and after which he carefully put them in bags again, fell asleep, and snored as before.

Jack crept quietly from his hiding-place, and approached the giant, when a little dog under the chair barked furiously. Much to his surprise, the giant slept on soundly, and the dog ceased. Jack seized the bags, reached the door in safety, and soon arrived at the bottom of the bean-stalk. When he reached his mother's cottage, he found it quite deserted. Full of astonishment he ran into the village, and an old woman directed him to a house, where he

found his mother apparently dying. On
being told of our hero's safe return,
his mother revived and soon recovered.
Jack then presented two bags of gold
and silver to her.

His mother saw that something
preyed upon his mind heavily, and

tried to find out the cause; but Jack
knew too well what the consequence
would be should he discover the cause
of his melancholy to her. He did his
utmost therefore to conquer the great
desire which now forced itself upon him
in spite of himself for another journey
up the bean-stalk, but in vain.

On the longest day Jack arose as soon
as it was light, climbed the bean-stalk,
and reached the top with some little
trouble. He found the road, journey,
etc., the same as before. He arrived at
the giant's house in the evening, and
found his wife standing as usual at the
door. Jack now appeared a different
character, and had disguised himself so
completely that she did not appear to
remember him. However, when he
begged admittance, he found it very
difficult to persuade her. At last he

prevailed, was allowed to go in, and was hidden in the copper.

When the giant returned, he said, as usual : "Wife ! wife ! I smell fresh meat ! " But Jack felt quite composed, as he had said so before, and had soon been satisfied.   However,   the   giant

started up suddenly, and notwithstanding
all his wife could say, he searched all
round the room. Whilst this was going
forward, Jack was much terrified, and
ready to die with fear, wishing himself
at home a thousand times ; but when the
giant approached the copper, and put his
hand upon the lid, Jack thought his
death was certain. Fortunately the giant
ended his search there, without moving
the lid, and seated himself quietly by the
fireside.

When the giant's supper was over,

he commanded his wife to fetch down his harp. Jack peeped under the copper-lid, and soon saw the most beautiful one that could be imagined. It was put by the giant on the table, who said : " Play," and it instantly played of its own accord. The music was uncommonly fine. Jack was delighted, and felt more anxious to get the harp into his possession than either of the former treasures.

The giant's soul was not attuned to harmony, and the music soon lulled him into a sound sleep. Now, therefore, was the time to carry off the harp, as the giant appeared to be in a more profound sleep than usual. Jack soon made up his mind, got out of the copper, and seized the harp ; which, however, being enchanted by a fairy, called out loudly : " Master, master ! "

The giant awoke, stood up, and tried to pursue Jack ; but he had drank so much that he could not stand. Jack ran as quick as he could. In a little time the giant was well enough to walk slowly, or rather to reel after him.

Had he been sober, he must have over-taken Jack instantly ; but as he then was, Jack contrived to be first at the top of the bean-stalk. The giant called to him all the way along the road in a voice like thunder, and was sometimes very near to him.

The moment Jack got down the bean-stalk, he called out for a hatchet : one was brought him directly.   Just at that instant the giant began to descend, but Jack with his hatchet cut the bean-stalk close off at the root, and the giant fell headlong into the garden. The fall instantly killed him.

Jack heartily begged his mother's pardon for all the sorrow and affliction he had caused her, promising most faithfully to be dutiful and obedient to her in future. He proved as good as his word, and became a pattern of affectionate behaviour and attention to his parent.